HERGÉ

THE ADVENTURES OF TINTIN

THE BLUE LOTUS

JOY STREET BOOKS

LITTLE, BROWN AND COMPANY

BOSTON/TORONTO/LONDON

HISTORICAL NOTE

Hergé first published *Le Lotus Bleu* in the magazine *Le Petit Vingtième* in Brussels in 1934-5: the story itself is set in 1931. At that time Japanese troops were occupying parts of the Chinese mainland, and Shanghai, the great seaport at the mouth of the Yangtze Kiang, possessed an International Settlement, a trading base in China for Western nations, administered by the British and Americans. Hergé based his narrative freely upon the events of the time, including the blowing-up of the South Manchurian railway, which led to further incursions by Japan into China and ultimately to Japan's resignation from the League of Nations in 1933.

Translated by Leslie Lonsdale-Cooper
and Michael Turner

The TINTIN books are published in the following languages :

Afrikaans :		HUMAN & ROUSSEAU, Cape Town.
Arabic :		DAR AL-MAAREF, Cairo.
Basque :		MENSAJERO, Bilbao.
Brazilian :		DISTRIBUIDORA RECORD, Rio de Janeiro.
Breton :		CASTERMAN, Paris.
Catalan :		JUVENTUD, Barcelona.
Chinese :		EPOCH, Taipei.
Danish :		CARLSEN IF, Copenhagen.
Dutch :		CASTERMAN, Dronten.
English :	U.K. :	METHUEN CHILDREN'S BOOKS, London.
	Australia :	OCTOPUS AUSTRALIA, Melbourne.
	Canada :	OCTOPUS CANADA, Toronto.
	New Zealand :	OCTOPUS NEW ZEALAND, Auckland.
	Republic of South Africa :	STRUIK BOOK DISTRIBUTORS, Johannesburg.
	Singapore :	OCTOPUS ASIA, Singapore.
	Spain :	EDICIONES DEL PRADO, Madrid.
	Portugal :	EDICIONES DEL PRADO, Madrid.
	U.S.A.	ATLANTIC, LITTLE BROWN, Boston.
Esperanto :		CASTERMAN, Paris.
Finnish :		OTAVA, Helsinki.
French :		CASTERMAN, Paris-Tournai.
	Spain :	EDICIONES DEL PRADO, Madrid.
	Portugal :	EDICIONES DEL PRADO, Madrid.
Galician :		JUVENTUD, Barcelona.
German :		CARLSEN, Reinbek-Hamburg.
Greek :		ANGLO-HELLENIC, Athens.
Icelandic :		FJÖLVI, Reykjavik.
Indonesian :		INDIRA, Jakarta.
Iranian :		MODERN PRINTING HOUSE, Teheran.
Italian :		GANDUS, Genoa.
Japanese :		FUKUINKAN SHOTEN, Tokyo.
Korean :		UNIVERSAL PUBLICATIONS, Seoul.
Malay :		SHARIKAT UNITED, Pulau Pinang.
Norwegian :		SEMIC, Oslo.
Picard :		CASTERMAN, Paris.
Portuguese :		CENTRO DO LIVRO BRASILEIRO, Lisboa.
Provençal :		CASTERMAN, Paris.
Spanish :		JUVENTUD, Barcelona.
	Argentina :	JUVENTUD ARGENTINA, Buenos Aires.
	Mexico :	MARIN, Mexico.
	Peru :	DISTR. DE LIBROS DEL PACIFICO, Lima.
Serbo-Croatian :		DECJE NOVINE, Gornji Milanovac
Swedish :		CARLSEN IF, Stockholm.
Welsh :		GWASG Y DREF WEN, Cardiff.

Artwork © 1946 by Casterman, Paris and Tournai

Library of Congress Catalogue Card Number Afor 5851

Artwork © renewed 1974 by Casterman
Library of Congress Catalogue Card Number R 585356

Translation Text © 1983 by Methuen & Co., Ltd., London
American Edition © 1984 by Little, Brown and Company (Inc.), Boston

Library of Congress catalog card no. 83-82204

ISBN 0-316-35891-6
10 9 8 7 6 5 4 3 2 1

Joy Street Books are published
by Little, Brown and Company (Inc.)

Published pursuant to agreement with Casterman, Paris
Not for sale in the British Commonwealth

Printed by Casterman, S.A., Tournai, Belgium.

THE BLUE LOTUS
藍蓮花

TINTIN AND SNOWY are in India, guests of the Maharaja of Gaipajama, enjoying a well-earned rest. The evil gang of international drug-smugglers, encountered in *Cigars of the Pharaoh*, has been smashed and its members are behind bars. With one exception. Only the mysterious gang-leader is unaccounted for: he disappeared over a cliff.

But questions have still to be answered. What of the terrible Rajaijah juice, the 'poison of madness'? Where were the shipments of opium going, hidden in the false cigars? And who really was the master-mind behind the operation?

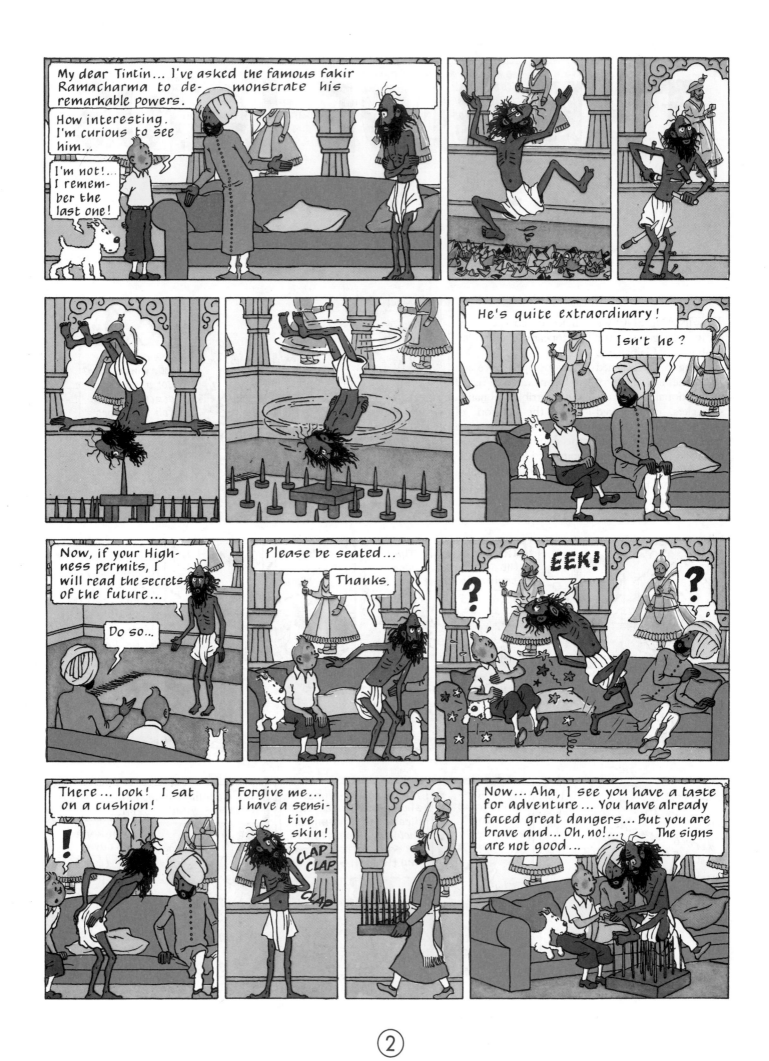

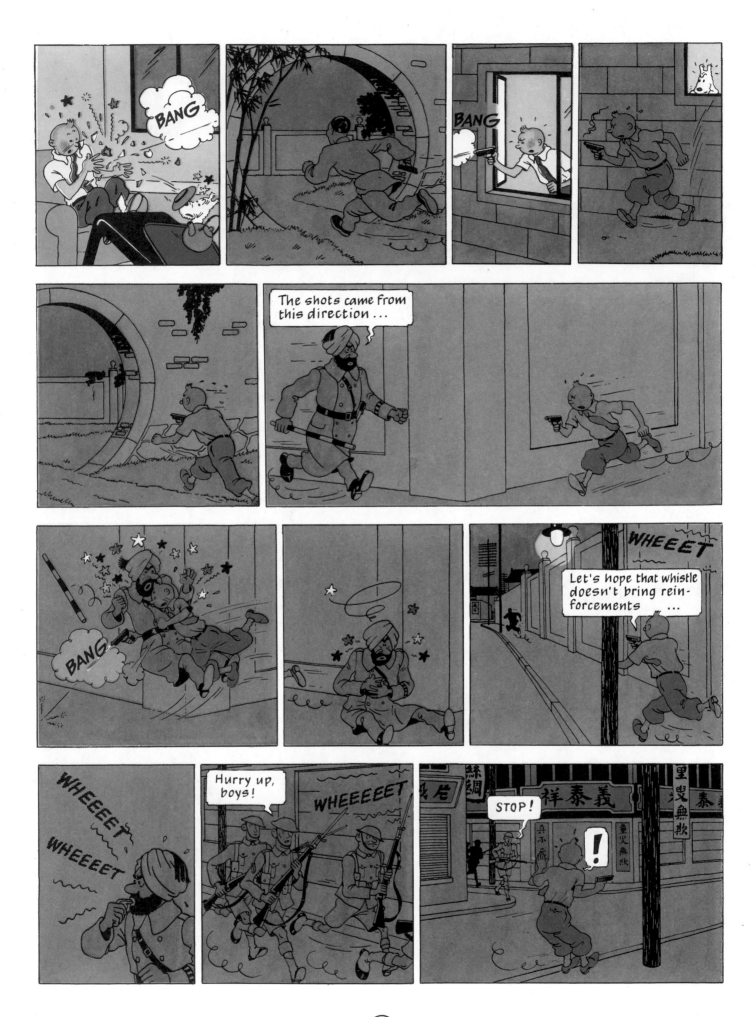

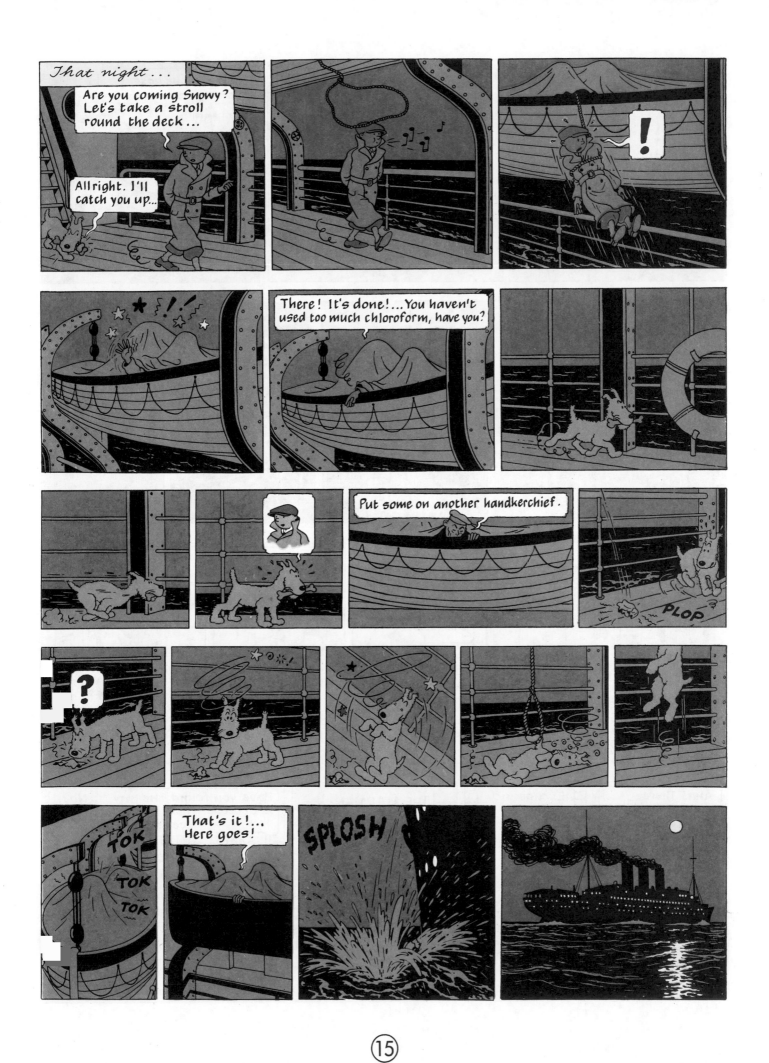

(1) See Cigars of the Pharaoh

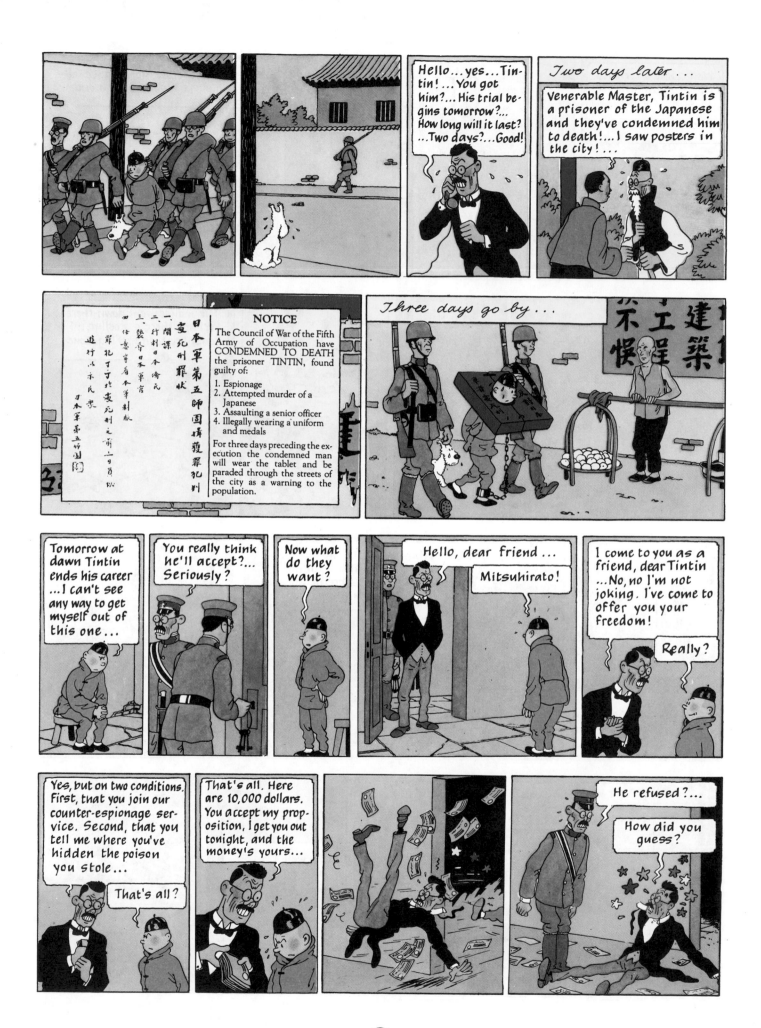

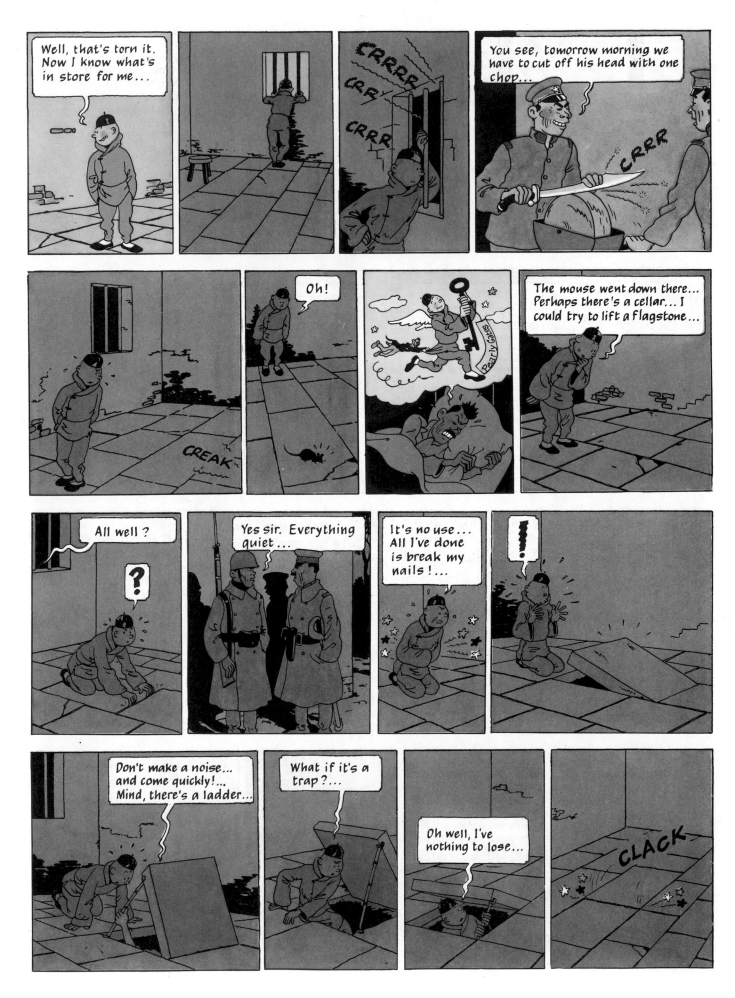

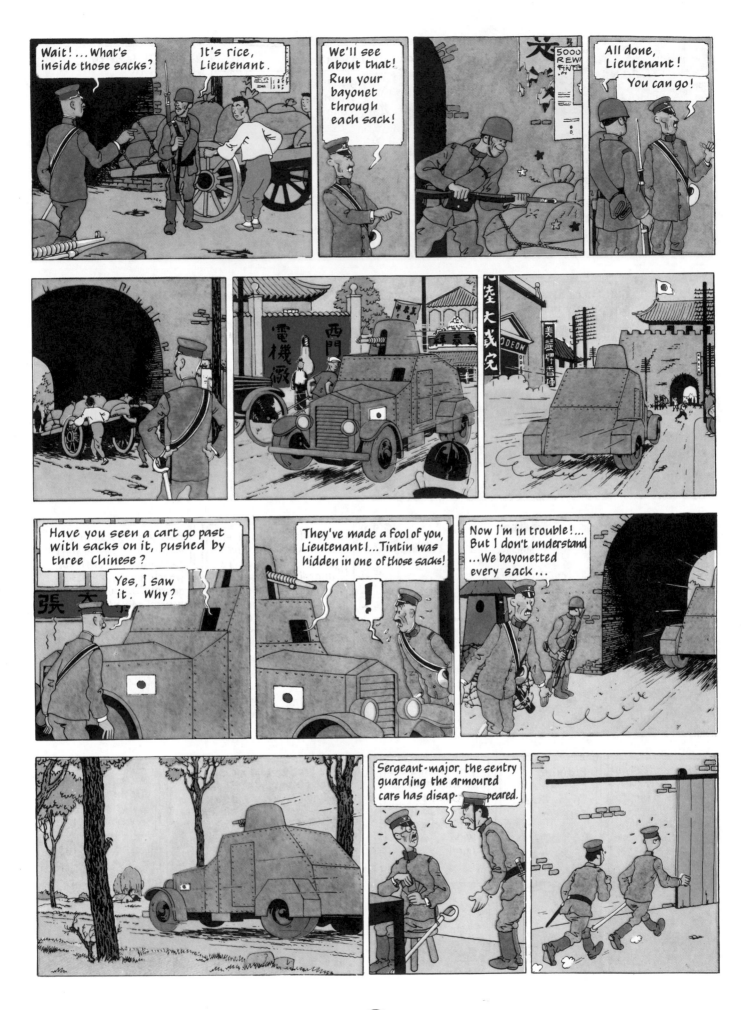

He's alive!

That's better, eh? You almost swallowed half the river!...What's your name?...I'm Tintin...

I am Chang Chong-chen...But ...why did you save my life?

?

I thought all white devils were wicked, like those who killed my grandfather and grandmother long ago. During the War of Righteous and Harmonious Fists, my father said.

The Boxer Rebellion, yes.

But Chang, all white men aren't wicked. You see, different peoples don't know enough about each other. Lots of Europeans still believe ...

...that all Chinese are cunning and cruel and wear pigtails, are always inventing tortures, and eating rotten eggs and swallows' nests...

The same stupid Europeans are quite convinced that all Chinese have tiny feet, and even now little Chinese girls suffer agonies with bandages...

...designed to prevent their feet developing normally. They're even convinced that Chinese rivers are full of unwanted babies, thrown in when they are born.

So you see Chang, that's what lots of people believe about China!

They must be crazy people in your country!!

Meanwhile...

I have news for you, General, about Tintin...

You know where he is?

I have just received a telegram... He caught a train this morning for Hukow...

Hukow?...But that's deep into Chinese territory. So long as he's there we can't touch him...

Excuse me, General, there is one way ...It's this...

Now, Chang, what are you going to do?

My parents are lost... I've nowhere to go... Couldn't I come with you?...

It's just... I may be running into great danger...

But two of us would be far stronger...

OK, then!... Off to Hukow!

I know a short cut ...

43

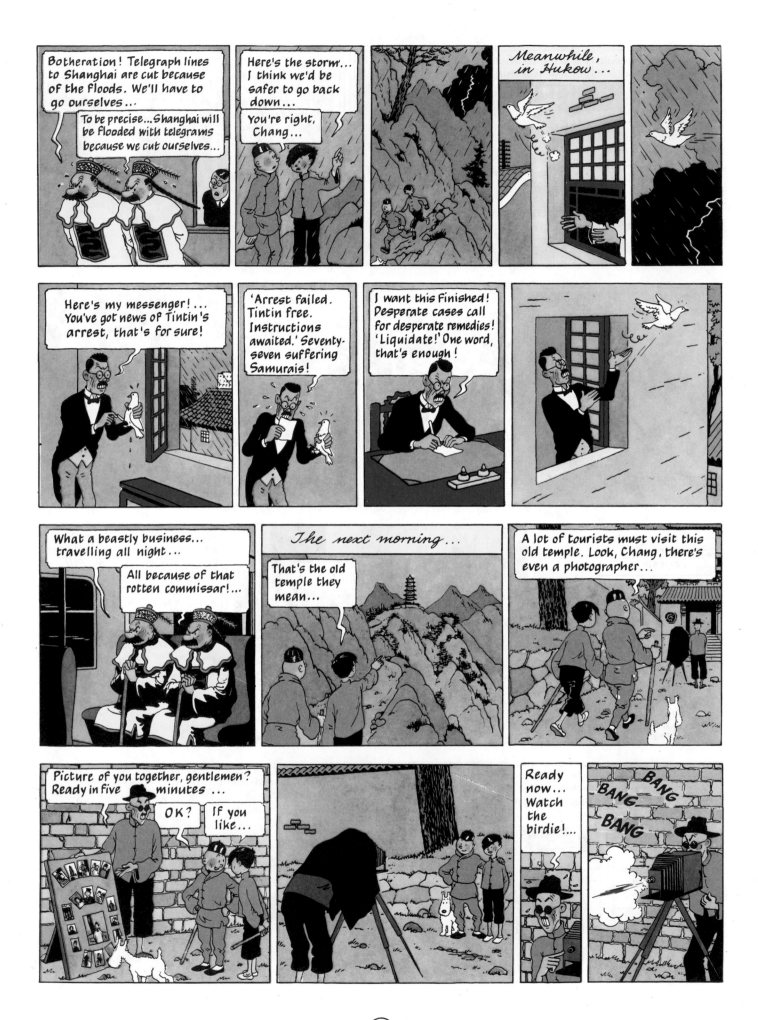

Something tells me you weren't expecting this sort of reception when you emerged!

Too true!

I knew perfectly well you were in the barrel...You were at the Blue Lotus last night ...and had a good laugh at my expense, no doubt... You heard the orders I gave Yamato... Everything had gone your way... But one of my men saw you leave and alerted me.

I told myself you certainly wouldn't be able to resist such a good opportunity, so I set a trap. I told them to leave you alone, they loosened the top of one barrel, and everything happened as I'd foreseen!

Well done, Mr Mitsuhirato. You're quite a clever man!

Cleverer than you thought, anyway!... Ah, here's an old friend of yours... He doesn't want to miss your execution!...

?

We got him, Grand Master.

Mr Rastapopoulos!

Exactly!

Rastapopoulos!...Roberto Rastapopoulos! You've been trying to spike my guns for a long time... Me, Rastapopoulos, king of drug smugglers...Rastapopoulos, who went over a cliff near Gaipajama...and you thought I died... Rastapopoulos, alive and well... And as always, coming out on top...

You, leader of the gang?... Impossible!

Bring in the others, Yamato...

You aren't convinced, eh?... Look at that!... Now do you believe me?...

The sign of the Pharaoh Kih-Oskh! (1)

Here, take this. It's for you...

Lao Tzu said: 'You must find the way. ... I've found it...It's quite easy. I'm going to cut off your head. Then you too will know the truth ...

You're...you're absolutely sure there isn't any risk for us?...

No, as soon as he's done the job Yamato will take care of him...

(1) See *Cigars of the Pharaoh*

SHANGHAI NEWS
上海報

FANG HSI-YING FOUND: Professor Prisoner in Opium Den

SHANGHAI, Wednesday: Professor Fang Hsi-ying has been found! The good news was flashed to us this morning.

Last week eminent scholar Fang disappeared on his way home from a party given by a friend. Police efforts to trace him were unavailing. No clues were found.

Professor Fang Hsi-ying pictured just after his release.

Young European reporter Tintin joined in the hunt for the missing man of science. Earlier we reported incidents involving Tintin and the occupying Japanese forces. Secret society Sons of the Dragon aided Tintin in the rescue. Fang Hsi-ying was kidnapped by an international gang of drug smugglers, now all safely in police custody.

A wireless transmitter was found by police at Blue Lotus opium den. The transmitter was used by the drug smugglers to communicate with their ships on the high seas. Information radioed included sea routes, ports to be avoided, points of embarkation and unloading.

Home of Japanese subject Mitsuhirato was also searched. No comment, say police on reports of seizure of top-secret documents. Unconfirmed rumours suggest the papers concern undercover political activity by a neighbouring power. Speculation mounts that they disclose recent Shanghai-Nanking railway incident as a pretext for extended Japanese occupation. League of Nations officials in Geneva will study the captured documents.

_____

TINTIN'S OWN STORY

This morning, hero of the hour Mr Tintin, talked to us about his adventures.

The young reporter is the guest of Mr Wang Chen-yee at his host's picturesque villa on the Nanking road. When we

Tintin, rescuer of Professor Fang Hsi-ying, with Snowy, his faithful companion.

called, our hero, young and smiling, greeted us wearing Chinese dress. Could this really be the scourge of the terrible Shanghai gangsters?

After our greetings and congratulations, we asked Mr Tintin to tell us how he succeeded in smashing the most dangerous organisation.

Mr Wang, a tall, elderly, venerable man with an impish smile said:

"You must tell the world it is entirely due to him that my wife, my son and I are alive today!"

With these words our interview was concluded, and we said farewell to the friendly reporter and his kindly host.

L.G.T.

Young people carry posters of Tintin through Shanghai streets.